Watch for these titles coming up in the
Choose Your Own Adventure® series.

Ask your bookseller for books you have missed
or visit us at cyoa.com to learn more.

PROJECT UFO

BY R. A. MONTGOMERY

ILLUSTRATED BY VLADIMIR SEMIONOV
COVER ILLUSTRATED BY MARCO CANNELLA

CHOOSE YOUR OWN ADVENTURE® CLASSICS
A DIVISION OF

CHOOSECO®
WAITSFIELD, VERMONT

Illustrated by: Vladimir Semionov
Cover illustrated by: Marco Cannella
Book design: Stacey Hood, Big Eyedea Visual Design

For information regarding permission, write to:

CHOOSECO

P.O. Box 46
Waitsfield, Vermont 05673
www.cyoa.com

ISBN-10: 1-933390-27-1
ISBN-13: 978-1-933390-27-7

Published simultaneously in the United States and Canada

Printed in the United States of America

0 9 8 7 6 5 4 3 2 1

BEWARE and WARNING!

This book is different from other books.

You and YOU ALONE are in charge of what happens in this story.

There are dangers, choices, adventures and consequences. YOU must use all of your numerous talents and much of your enormous intelligence. The wrong decision could end in disaster—even death. But, don't despair. At anytime, YOU can go back and make another choice, alter the path of your story, and change its result.

You have spent your life communicating telepathically with a trusted friend named Freedo. You know very little about Freedo's life, but you sense that your conversations are becoming increasingly important—not only for Freedo's planet, but for Earth as well! Freedo is sending you messages about the galaxy Calax III. You've never heard of it, but when you try to get more information, Freedo won't answer! Now different groups of Earth scientists have started asking you some suspicious questions. How can you help Freedo—and the Earth—survive?

"Are you there? This is Freedo. I'm in trouble. I need your—" The communication goes dead. You try your best to clear your mind and let Freedo tune in again. Finally, you hear his voice, loud and clear. "I fear Calax III. Beware . . ." Then silence again.

Ever since you were five years old you have been talking to Freedo and his companions. At first you would be woken up during your afternoon nap by high-pitched whining sounds like the buzz of mosquitoes. They would occur almost every day, so you began to really pay attention to them. After a while you could hear distinct voices. Soon the voices spoke your language, or maybe you spoke theirs. It didn't really matter—you could understand each other.

When you first told your parents about the sounds, they didn't believe you. And when you told them about the voices, they brought you to old Dr. Muleskin, who asked you some silly questions and prescribed lots of fruit juice and no TV for a month. This taught you a quick lesson: be patient with adults. They think they know everything, but they really don't.

Turn to the next page.

Several years ago, you asked Freedo, "When are you guys coming down for a visit?"

"Actually, we are visiting right now. You can't see us, but we're working on it."

"Wow. No wonder there have been so many sightings lately. . . . Hey, how come you guys show up in flying saucers?"

"My dear friend, those aren't our saucers, as you call them. They may be from Calax III, a planet of warriors and thieves who send attack teams to planets throughout the galaxy. They've been working on new ways to attack. Beware."

Since then, you and Freedo have become very close friends. He's always been there to help you with your problems. Now Freedo needs help, and you'd like to be there for him. But there's no way you can get in touch with him. You stare at the walls of your bedroom, which are covered with star charts. You feel helpless.

It's no wonder you've become a big science

buff, particularly in "intelligent" communication from outer space. Governments around the world have huge dish antennae focused on the heavens to pick up any signals. There's one in New Mexico called the Very Large Array. Every now and then, some group claims to have found a message but can't decipher it. Some scientists believe it's all just background noise in the universe caused by stars, supernovas, comets, and black holes. Others say it's just a coincidence and there are no messages at all. But of course you know better.

Two years ago you decided to join a small group of amateur astronomers working out of a small observatory. With the help of Freedo, you've been able to offer your team some valuable tips. You would like to tell them about Freedo and Calax III— it would be such a scientific breakthrough—but you know you have to be cautious.

Turn to page 5.

"Adios, Freedo," you shout and begin to make tracks for the door. There is no sense in getting involved. As you reach for the door— zap!

You can't move. You are locked in a state of suspended animation.

"That should hold you until I'm through with this creep," Suprana chortles. "It could be a long, long time. Enjoy."

The End

Recently your astronomy team has gained quite a reputation in scientific circles. Freedo had given you some information about deep space radiation levels and the nature of black holes. You compiled the information into a report for your astronomy group. They were so impressed they submitted it to the National Science Times. Since then the phone has been ringing off the hook with bigwigs from Washington, D.C., Palo Alto, England, Russia, and China. Suddenly you've become a minor big deal.

Turn to the next page.

During your lunch hour at school one day, you are met by three people, two women and a man, who claim to be government agents from the Center for Galactic Research.

"We want you to join our research efforts at our Boulder, Colorado facility," one of them announces. "We are probing what we believe are messages from outer space. We need young people with open, inquiring minds. It will be a lot of desk work, a lot of time in front of a computer, but you could make an important contribution to our world. We believe we are on to something big."

"I'll think it over," you reply. You don't know why you hesitate. Their credentials look real, but some inner feeling makes you a little suspicious of the whole thing. You wonder what the government is really interested in. However, this could be a way to get in touch with Freedo. Their equipment could be of great help.

Turn to the next page.

8

That night, you get a telephone call from another group—a nongovernmental agency called the LifeCom for Intelligent Life Studies, dedicated to flying saucer research. This group is supported by wealthy individuals from around the world who reject government involvement in scientific research. They realize the government is well-established and committed to its efforts, but they think it also keeps important information from the public.

Go on to the next page.

You decide to think about the offers from both groups overnight. You know the group of astronomers you've been working with doesn't have the facilities you need to help Freedo. Maybe the government does know more than they're letting on and could lead you straight to your alien friend. Working for the government is a once-in-a-lifetime opportunity. But then again, you're not sure they can be trusted. The private group, with their focus on UFO research, might lead you to the Calax III craft, where Freedo might be held captive.

You wonder what your friend Freedo would recommend. Either way, if Freedo is really in danger, you've got to do something.

If you decide to join the government group, the Center for Galactic Research, and study deep space messages, turn to page 10.

If you decide to go with the private group, the LifeCom for Intelligent Life Studies, and work on flying saucer research, turn to page 15.

You decide to join the Center for Galactic Research.

Arrangements are made with your school for a special education release. You will get full credit and work with a tutor at the center. The opportunities will be fantastic, and hopefully you'll be a step nearer to finding Freedo.

A week later you are in Colorado. The front range of the Rockies stands out like a fence rising off the high plains. Boulder lies snuggled up to these beauties. The famous Flatirons with their broad, sunbathed faces of smooth rock overlook the town. Bill Pitting, the director of the center, and Holly Hayworth, the head of your project, meet you at Denver's Stapleton Airport.

"Welcome to Colorado," Bill says, shaking your hand vigorously. He has a lanky physique and a strong handshake.

"Thanks. I can't wait—"

Turn to the next page.

But you hardly get an opportunity to talk. Bill just rambles on a mile a minute about frequencies, radio signal emission rates, radioactive decay—so much that your head spins. As Bill turns the car into the main entrance of the government complex, Holly turns to you and says, "I'm really glad you're here. We have set up a special office for you."

Something about her seems very familiar, but you know you've never seen her before. She keeps on talking, explaining the different projects and the equipment. Then you realize it's her voice that you know. You concentrate on placing the way she speaks, her words, her grammar, her tone. Then you hit it: messages that you received from Calax III when you and Freedo were eavesdropping on their frequencies were similar in tone. But that's impossible, you think.

Then she asks, innocently enough, "Have you ever heard of Plaxton?"

Instantly you are on guard. You shake your head.

But you have heard of Plaxton. You think it's the name of a Calax III base that Freedo has been trying to pinpoint. You can't be sure, though.

Go on to the next page.

"Well, it's not important," she continues. "If you ever need special help or aid, I'm right down the hall."

Your instincts scream at you to scrambolino right now! Holly's voice sounds so similar to the Calax III transmissions that you're starting to freak. On the other hand, you wonder if you're just imagining things or having a strange case of *déjà vu*.

If you follow your instincts and flee right now, turn to page 22.

If you hold the course and stay, turn to page 35.

Your decision to join the LifeCom for Intelligent Life Studies is greeted with great pleasure by the group's executive body—Sanram Sing-dop, Hellod Fergio, Melton Dunkways, and Marlene Fitz.

In a massive dining room at the mansion of Marlene Fitz you are introduced to many notable space physicists, biologists, and theoretical mathematicians.

"Welcome to our group," Fitz says, holding up a glass of wheat-grass juice. "We are dedicated to making room on our planet for all beings regardless of their planet of origin. May you thrive in our company and we in yours."

Suddenly there is a scraping of chairs. All present hurl their empty glasses into the roaring fire in the huge fireplace.

This is all very odd to you, but when Marlene Fitz commands, "Now you." You obey and throw your glass into the blaze.

Turn to the next page.

16

You spend the night in a room bigger than your whole house. A butler named Winder serves you breakfast in bed. You are very careful not to spill the maple syrup onto the blankets.

"Madame has arranged the helicopter for you this morning," Winder announces in a British accent.

"Fine. Tell the pilot to stand by for his passenger," you reply, playing along.

"As you wish," Winder says and struts off.

Later that morning you are taken in the helicopter to a small field where a private jet awaits you. Hours later you land below a remote mountain laboratory up in the Sangre de Cristo mountains outside Santa Fe, New Mexico. Everyone you have come into contact with this morning wears an olive-green uniform. There are no insignia on the uniforms, but the people—pilots, mechanics, and ground crew—all behave like well-trained soldiers.

You are now being driven up the mountain in a 4 x 4 vehicle. No one talks. You feel uncomfortable.

Turn to the next page.

Finally you reach a well-hidden concrete building of modern design snugged up to the outcropping rock. It blends in so well with its surroundings that you barely notice it.

Silently you are passed on to three other uniformed agents and taken to a massive observatory or control room. A handful of people in civilian clothes are huddled around a large, oval-shaped table. Computers and banks of electronic gear crowd the surrounding walls. Uniformed technicians operate these machines. An air of expectancy and tension permeates the entire room.

Looking upward to the ceiling, you see a grid of the world. Coordinates and major grid lines are marked in glowing red. At several spots are blinking yellow lights.

"There. See it?" comes a stern and excited voice. "I knew it would be back."

You don't wonder for long what they are talking about as an overhead holographic projector creates the image of a longish cylinder with a large round plate attached to its midsection. The cylinder is punctuated by portholes and glows with an intense silver light.

This is a UFO. You wonder where on Earth it has been spotted and photographed.

Turn to the next page.

"Come here, recruit," says the same stern, excited voice. "You are in for a special treat today. See that saucer up there?" he asks, pointing to the hologram.

"Yes, sir," you reply. This certainly isn't what you expected. The whole organization seems like some paramilitary organization. You wonder what you have gotten yourself into.

"Good. We'll arrange for old Bernie—that's what we call that old-timer—to pick you up. How does that sound? Or, there are other ways to get initiated."

"What's up with this initiation?" you ask, completely annoyed now.

"Oh, nobody told you about it? Well, aren't you in for a nice surprise? Why not try Bernie? It's that or . . . I'll come up with another choice." The voice chuckles.

*If you decide to go with Bernie,
go on to the next page.*

*If you give Bernie a pass and decide to wait for
another "initiation" option, turn to page 45.*

"I guess I'll try Bernie," you reply.

There is a round of applause and a low level of laughter.

"Good for you. We knew we'd picked the right one. Now, go out to the launch pad, install yourself in the transporter pod, activate Program NB3, and sit back. Have a nice trip."

It is windy out on the launch pad, but you approach the egg-shaped transporter, examine it briefly, open the hatch, and climb inside. Instructions above the hatch tell you to fasten the six holding bolts, turn the locking wheel to the right, and initiate the preprogrammed launch code.

You hesitate and then just do it. You try to relax as you wait to see what happens.

Turn to page 30.

"I'm out of here," you say to yourself. You figure you'll wait until dark, when everyone's asleep. Then you can sneak out and make for the bus station. Meanwhile, you have to remain polite and try not to let anyone know about your plan of escape.

For the next hour, Holly shows you around the building and finally to your office. Once you see the amazing view of the Rockies from the floor-to-ceiling window and the high-tech computer and your very own telephone, you almost forget about your plans to leave. Imagining yourself as an important government agent, you can't help but chuckle.

Holly gives you a long, penetrating look. "Sometimes I feel the best time to search the universe is during the early morning hours. Earth is so quiet then; we can really concentrate. Don't you agree?" she asks.

"Sure. Early morning, great time," you blurt out.

"Fine. We'll meet in my office at 3:00 AM. Might as well start off right," she says in a quiet, commanding tone.

You feel as if she has probed your brain and knows everything about you—including your fears and your plan of escape. Claustrophobia of the worst kind hits you. A radical shift in timing is needed. You have to get out of here.

Turn to the next page.

But first you have to get to a phone to alert your parents and find out the bus schedule. You don't want to use your office phone in case it's bugged. Fortunately, you are able to find two pay phones just outside the building. One is out of service, and the other is being used by a fat man, who jiggles when he talks. He just chatters away as if nobody was waiting.

Annoyed, you wait for what seems like forever. Then it happens. The fat man turns, and you suddenly realize he has no face. There is only a flat plastic disc where his face should be. You think you must be dreaming.

"There will be no more faces for you, now or ever," the faceless one says to you. "I have come to take specimens from this forbidden planet. You look like a fine one. Let's go."

With a flick of his wrist, you are engulfed in a cloud of greenish gas and taken away from the time and place you know so well. The voice is familiar. It is a Calax III voice.

Turn to the next page.

26

"Let go of me!" you shout with all your force. But it does no good. You are already high above the Earth. Your speed increases, so that you seem to be exiting the orbit of planets and zooming by stars faster than the speed of light.

"Where are we going? Who are you?" you ask.

The creature has changed form now. It resembles a glowing orb. Strangely, you experience no real fear, only a muted curiosity at what is happening to you.

Suddenly and without warning, the trip ends! Light turns to dark. With a swooshing sound, you and the light blob descend into a vortex of light and movement. It feels as if you're going down a roller coaster in slow motion. A low rumble, half music, half noise, emanates from the center of the vortex. You like it; it's soothing. But you wish the creature would communicate somehow.

Turn to the next page.

"Where are we?" you demand.

"We are where we should be. Don't ask foolish questions. All will be revealed, in time." The form becomes silent again and then begins another transformation. It dims, reduces in size, and becomes almost opaque.

A room appears. It seems like any other normal room. But as you examine it, you realize the room has no boundaries. No entrances and no exits. It is as if the concept of dimension does not exist here.

A sense of familiarity intensifies for just a moment and then vanishes.

"Are you ready?" chimes a voice.

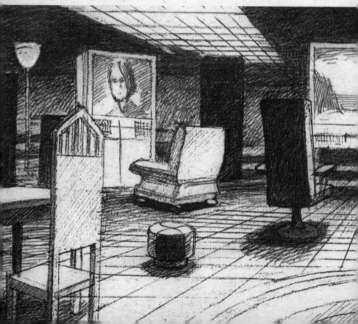

"Ready? Ready for what?" you reply, surprised that you are not frightened.

"Don't play games. You have tempted the fates—you have lured us to pick you up. Are you ready?"

You scan your memory, trying to come up with some instance when you might have tempted the fates. Maybe you played too many video games, and now some creature from the deepest tunnels has emerged to get you. No, that's foolish, you tell yourself. This is probably just a dream.

Turn to page 36.

In the blink of an eye, you and your transporter are hurled into the afternoon sky with a rocketlike force.

You are so busy holding on, you do not notice at first that the instruments on the port wall are all off their scales. You are making tracks. But to where?

Your transporter comes to a wrenching halt beneath an enormous brown pad. Gaping mechanical jaws are spread wide in welcome. A tractor beam pulls you inside. The great jaws close. Darkness envelops you.

Turn to the next page.

For what seems like an eternity, you wait and worry. You realize that all your dreams of making contact with UFOs are now being met. Or else this is just another wild dream. Maybe you'll wake up in your nice warm bed in your nice messy room.

Fat chance. This is no dream, and you know it.

Go on to the next page.

At last there is some activity. First lights, then sounds. At first they are disturbing to you, but as they persist you find them almost pleasing. Maybe you are being hypnotized. Then your transporter is pried open by a laser beam, and you fall unceremoniously to the floor of this giant flying object.

"Throw this puny offering to the wolves!" The command echoes in the giant docking hangar.

Three robots approach. Two grasp you by the arms, and you are hauled away to be tossed to the wolves.

The other robot, only two steps in front of you, leads the way. You see a weapon of some sort dangling from its side. You feel the urge to reach for it. This might be your only chance. On the other hand, you're completely surrounded by superstrong robots.

If you reach for the weapon, turn to page 37.

If you wait for a better chance, turn to page 43.

You decide to stay for the time being. And as Pitting and Holly show you around, nothing seems especially out of the ordinary. You might even have a lot of fun here.

"Great. I really like this office. Kids don't usually get to have their own offices," you say, spinning yourself around in the swivel leather chair. You're amazed at the fantastic view you have of the Rockies from the floor-to-ceiling window. And your very own telephone and computer!

"Well, out here we don't see any difference between kids and adults. It's performance that counts, and you've got the smarts. At least, that's what I hear. Deal?" Pitting says, holding out his hand.

"Deal," you reply, shaking his hand.

Oddly, Holly does not shake. She moves quickly on to her office. "See you tomorrow," she says.

Pitting opens up your desk and explains the communication system and the computer link. You have the new 3D screen and voice-activated Internet connection.

"People from dozens of countries are all trying to get in contact with other cosmic civilizations. One argument explaining the lack of contact so far is that if we, as civilized human beings, can't carry on comprehensive dialogues with whales and dolphins, then how do we expect to communicate with extraterrestrials?"

Turn to page 39.

But you realize the voice is waiting for an answer. You feel it closing in on you. What if you just ignored it, you wonder. This could be just a game.

If you decide to follow the voice,
turn to page 48.

If you decide to ignore the voice,
turn to page 38.

Quickly you extricate your left arm from the robot's grasp and lunge for the weapon. It is the last thing you remember doing. The instrument turns out not to be a weapon. Instead, it is a tool designed to disconnect all electrical circuits.

In a flash, you become a rather large puddle of water. Soon you evaporate and join the atmosphere as a part of the system that nourishes the Earth.

The End

You decide to ignore the voice. You wait. Nothing happens. No noise, no warmth, no light, nothing. Time has frozen, it seems, and with it space has retreated.

"SEND THIS ONE BACK. THIS ONE IS A REJECT."

"Hey, wait a minute," you yell. "I was only kidding. I'm ready to go now." You are amazed to hear yourself say this. You had wanted to go back home—and now's your chance. But to your surprise you are refusing.

"TOO LATE."

Suddenly you feel your body being sucked up through a dark vacuum. You feel as though you are suffocating. All your body functions are slowing down, even though you're traveling at an accelerating speed. Each moment seems to last forever. Childhood memories flow through your mind, calming you. You think about your parents and Freedo. Freedo! You remember your plan to rescue Freedo.

"What are you doing out here? We've got work to do." You realize Holly is talking to you. You're confused.

"Are you ready?" she asks.

For what? you wonder.

The End

You never really looked at it that way. To you communicating with aliens is no problem!

Interrupting your thoughts, Pitting says, "The offices are open twenty-four hours a day. You'll always find people here. I don't know what your work habits are, but don't worry. You do what works for you."

"Thanks, Dr. Pitting," you reply.

"Hey, none of that 'doctor' business. Call me Pitt."

Turn to the next page.

The day flies by, and by night sleep is a welcome relief. You are exhausted from all the new experiences. But at 2:22 A.M. you wake up. Something about Holly and the Calax III connection makes you uneasy and suspicious. Instinct urges you to check out your office.

You sneak out of your room in the thin light of a gibbous moon and make your way across the quadrangle between the housing section and the offices. The night watchman is barely awake and doesn't notice you.

The entrance to the office complex is spooky. There is a digital lock requiring three codes beginning with your own personal code, then a departmental code, then a random number generated daily and left on your personal voice mail. It takes you a few minutes to familiarize yourself with the system, but the lock finally yields.

Contrary to what Pitt said, there are no other people in the office at this hour. You wonder why but soon put the thought aside. The door to your office is ajar, and the computer is on!

"What's going on?" you exclaim out loud. Your voice echoes in the empty office.

"Don't be afraid. Keep calm. Talk in a low whisper," comes a command. It seems to be coming right from the computer.

"Who are you?" you manage to squeak.

Turn to the next page.

"You've forgotten already?" comes the reply.

"Freedo! It's you. Freedo, you're back," you rejoice.

"Sorry to have been away for so long. I'll explain later. Right now . . ."

A shadow falls across your desk. Slowly you turn to look up into Holly's face. She does not smile.

"Who were you talking to?" she asks.

"Myself," you reply, thinking quickly. "Just talking out loud."

"Quite a conversation, I'd say. Let's take a look at your computer."

"Well, it's really nothing," you continue, reaching over and clicking the computer off. You hope that Freedo has gotten the message.

"I think you're hiding something," Holly continues. "Want to tell me?"

Why would you want to confide in Holly about Freedo? But then again she might be well connected and able to lead you to Freedo. You don't know what to do—you can't stand the way she's glaring at you.

If you confide in her about Freedo,
turn to page 80.

If you decide not to tell her about Freedo,
turn to page 44.

You decide to wait for a better chance to escape and in the meantime to play it cool. No sense in making a move at this point.

The robots take you inside the flying saucer to a compartment that seems to be some sort of electronic decontaminating room. You are subjected to high-pitched sounds and beams of light. The robots seem to giggle at you.

Once all the decontaminating is done, the robots stop laughing. They march you to a light-beam escalator—which is more like a conveyor belt—and toss you to its mercies.

Zingo! With a rush and a bump you are deposited into the middle of a rectangular space with walls and floor covered with deep maroon velvet.

Checking your wristwatch, you find that it has been scrubbed clean of all digits. You chalk that up to the decontamination process.

A soft mechanical voice says, "Ready yourself for initial meetings."

You come to attention. This is it.

Turn to page 85.

44

"Well, Holly," you say, hoping you can throw her off-guard, "I actually do have a slight problem— I talk to myself. I don't really like to discuss it, though. You see, I've never considered it a serious problem. But it has always been a major concern for my parents. They think I'm sick or something. They've sent me to dozens of doctors, psychiatrists, psychologists, and everyone came up with a different diagnosis. Now they don't know what to do. For the time being they've just given up on the whole therapy thing."

You keep talking as fast as you can, hoping Holly will lose interest in you. This strategy usually works quite well with adults. "Actually, I'm really very normal. I'm up on hip hop, rap, soul, sports— just ask me anything about basketball, baseball, football, pro wrestling. . . . By the way, Holly, do you know anything about foot problems? That's one thing I need to learn more about. Can you imagine all the little bones that make up just one foot? I was watching this program on TV and—"

"Stop it! I've heard enough," Holly says.

Turn to page 61.

"I'd rather try another initiation test," you say.

"Okay. If you are serious about studying flying saucers, then you will no doubt agree to go out on a three-day mission to spot them."

"I don't quite understand," you reply.

"Not much to understand. You will be taken out and dropped off on a mesa far from any sign of civilization. We usually use one of the old Anasazi ruins for this type of thing."

"Then what?" you query.

"You simply spend three days and nights waiting for contact. You see, we know that they are out there waiting for us. Some, like good old Bernie, we know from long experience. But Bernie's crew is hard to communicate with. And frankly, we have lost some of our people to Bernie."

"Lost? What do you mean?" you ask.

"Just that. They don't come back. Although it might not be all bad, you know."

"So I'm to be some sort of guinea pig out on some forgotten mesa? Then what?"

"We shall see. You will not be unobserved. It's time to go."

Turn to the next page.

46

Like it or not, you are bundled into a Zoomer 4 x 4 and driven for three hours deep into the mesa country northwest of Santa Fe. The road narrows, eventually becoming a bumpy farm path designed for goats and sheep. The four-wheel-drive vehicle groans and strains over rocks and through dry streambeds as it climbs at a steep angle.

Che, the driver, doesn't say much, but you manage to get him to admit that he would never submit to three nights out on a search like this.

"You're a decoy, partner. Simple as hunting. They stick you out there and see who comes by to sniff." Che punctuates this statement with a snap of his chewing gum.

Two major turns, another stream to cross, up at a steep angle, and then Che stops the Zoomer.

Turn to page 49.

"Well, I'm ready—I guess. I mean, I don't know what I'm supposed to be ready for, but I'll take a chance." Your voice is thin and reedy. There is a sense of destiny in your response and a feeling of helplessness. You feel you no longer have any control over what might happen, so you just wait.

But nothing happens.

"Well, how about it? I can't wait forever, you know," you say.

"These things take time," the voice responds. "The trouble with you Earthlings is that you want everything right here and now. That just isn't always possible. Hold on. You don't want me to make a mistake, do you?"

"What do you mean 'mistake'?" you ask, envisioning some horrendous crash of a superduper electronic device that would turn you into a gigaflop of disconnections.

"Wait, I've almost got it!" The voice sounds quite positive and happy now. You also notice that the endless room has changed. It is now a self-duplicating, four-dimensional grid. On top of the grid is an overlay of color and music. You can actually see the music—it looks like syrup that pours down and coats part of the grid. It is colored like a neon lamp, but the colors keep shifting and changing. It's hypnotizing.

Turn to page 54.

"Well, there she is. Mesa Malcontenta. She's all yours." Che points upward to a steep, flat-topped mesa. "Here's a pack. You got some grub and a sleeping bag. There's a flashlight and some other stuff. See ya in three days. Good luck."

"But Che, what am I supposed to do?" you plead.

"Nothin'. Just wait. Build a fire, watch the smoke. Examine the old pueblo ruins. Watch for snakes. They can be your guide."

Turn to the next page.

He drives off. You put on your pack and start up the old trail to the top of the mesa. You can imagine Native Americans centuries ago hiking this very path with loads of wood or jugs of water, returning to their mesa retreat. High above the valley, they felt safe in their mud-brick homes. These ancient ones lived in a world far removed from yours. Now only remnants of their past exist.

The trail is steep, and the footing is not good. Finally you crest the hill, and before you spreads a flat surface with a few wind-twisted pinyon trees. The outlines of a pueblo greet you with silence. The walls on the north side still loom, showing where individual houses stood. The mud bricks look as though they were placed there only weeks before. Scoured by the wind and sun and rain, they are clean and beautiful.

The loneliness of the day overwhelms you, and sadness fills the void. Maybe you should retreat, go back down the hill, leave this spooky place of the past.

If you decide to leave, turn to page 52.

If you decide to stay, turn to page 71.

"I'm out of here," you shout to the wind and mountains and air. "I'm free."

Two strides, then three, and you are running, with joy and fear and a sense that time is on your side.

You stumble. Jagged rocks come rushing at you. You taste blood as it trickles down your face.

You rise slowly to your knees. There is a rustling sound. It becomes louder.

No, it's not a rustling; it is a rattling.

Eyes meet yours. A forked tongue flicks out to taste the wind, preparing the fangs.

The rattler suddenly transforms into a woman dressed in animal skins and cobwebs. Her smile reminds you of your mother when you were a small child. She comforts you and tells you stories of the beginning of life. You collect your energy and listen to her, realizing that her stories are the heart of all myth and the legends of all people.

The End

54

The colors are really swirling now. From light to dark, dark to spangles of silver and gold, spangles to starbursts, then starbursts to rainbows!

"Wow!" you exclaim. "This is some kind of cosmic MTV—like liquid TV. You're the DJ or the host or something. Right?"

"Wrong. That was just a malfunction. But don't worry—you'll be all right. I'll have her fixed in a jiffy," the voice answers.

The light show calms down, the music and colors fade, and things return to normal. It's like being inside on a boring, rainy day.

"Well, come on, I'm still waiting," you persist. "Freedo, where are you when I need you?" you mumble, hoping this creature isn't from Calax III.

"I think I've got it this time," the voice replies.

You are lifted up, turned around, and spun as though you were being puréed in a food processor. You feel yourself coming apart.

Go on to the next page.

"Well, maybe I don't have it yet. This isn't exactly what I had wanted," the voice says quietly.

"Exactly what did you want?" you ask, feeling terribly uncomfortable in your new disconnected state of being.

"To tell you the truth, I wasn't quite sure. I've never dealt with one of your type before. I'm new at this game. I mean, don't get upset or anything. . . . I'm what you would call an apprentice."

"Yikes! You mean to tell me you goons dragged me off to this forsaken spot and you don't even know what you want to do with me? Oh, Freedo, where are you?"

"Calm down. Calm down. Give me a break. I'm trying my best. So I'm a bit sloppy. I just need practice; nothing is ever perfect the first time," the being explains. "Do you know Freedo, too? I thought Freedo was a secret agent."

"Listen here, buddy, get my body back to normal, please. And hurry up. No mistakes this time," you order. You feel your anger rising.

"Okay! Okay! Hold your breath. I'll try," the voice says.

Turn to the next page.

While you are busy worrying, the voice begins to take shape. It looks amazingly like a scrawny kid you knew back in third grade. No, this can't be, you think to yourself. That kid, Aldo Archibald Fitmouse, was famous for being a klutz. You remember how he couldn't even open his lunch box without untying his shoelaces and dropping his cell phone.

Turn to the next page.

There is a smell of old sneakers burning, and then a bright flicker. Zump! You are back in one piece. Standing before you is a creature that looks like Aldo Fitmouse.

He turns to you with a big smile on his face. "See, I'm not so bad. I got you back together, didn't I?"

Suddenly you hear an entirely different voice that fills both of you with dread.

"ALDO. OH, ALDO. WHERE ARE YOU? ARE YOU FINISHED WITH THAT THING YOU DRAGGED HOME FROM THAT FILTHY PLANET EARTH?" it echoes.

Aldo begins to shrink right in front of you. His eyes radiate fear.

"Who's that, Aldo?" you ask, ignoring his latest transformation.

Go on to the next page.

"It's Lepodoptro. People call him Lepto for short. He's famous around here for torturing bugs and things. And he's always minding everyone else's business. Let's get out of here."

"Wait a minute, Aldo. Where can we go, and how do I get back home?"

"Oh, yeah, I forgot. You're a gloob from Earth. Well, you help me, and I'll help you."

"How?" you ask. Things are getting out of hand—now you are in the middle of a giant forest of trees with bright bluish foliage that looks metallic.

"You're nosy and impatient," Aldo replies. "I'll tell you exactly how you can help. But first you need to agree to a secret pact."

Turn to the next page.

"A secret pact? Are you nuts or something? We don't have time for a club meeting," you reply.

"Well, it's my way or no way. Lepto is coming, and he'll be furious. You'll only irritate him. And when he's mad, he's mad. So, it's the secret pact or face the consequences."

Now you're really annoyed. Why should you agree to some secret pact Aldo won't even tell you about?—he could be up to anything. You're tempted to just run away—far away. But as you look around, you're not so sure you want to make your escape in the giant metallic forest, especially with Lepto lurking about.

If you agree to this "secret pact," turn to page 65.

If you decide to try to escape, turn to page 79.

You blink and fix her with a surprised stare. Your tactic seems to work.

"So sorry I interrupted you," she says. She gives you a strange look, as if you're out of your mind. You're not sure whether she believes you or not, but she doesn't press you on the issue any further. "Go ahead with your conversation. I'm leaving. Oh, by the way, there seems to be heavy traffic in one sector of the universe headed this way," she adds, then pauses to see if you rise to the bait.

"You know, Holly, I'm so new at this game that I don't even know what you mean. Would you mind showing me? I mean, how do I get into this whole thing?" You look up at her again with wonder and expectation.

"Not now. I'm sorry, you'll just have to learn on your own." She storms out of the room, and you hear her footsteps retreating to the elevators at the end of the hallway.

"Thank heavens she's gone," you whisper.

"You can say that again," Freedo says.

"Boy, am I glad you're back. You really had me scared. I thought you were dead or something."

Turn to the next page.

"Well, to tell you the truth, I was," Freedo says in a solemn voice.

"You were what?" you say incredulously.

"I was dead. The Calax III mob got me and my crew in a fierce little intergalactic space battle. They jumped us—dry-gulched us, as I think you people call it."

"When? Where?" you ask.

Go on to the next page.

"Oh, you don't really want me to go through it all. You Earth people know more about wars and destruction than I can ever tell you. It's more humane—no pun intended—in space. Once they zapped us we just ceased to exist. Basically, they took over. They became us, and we became them. We were consumed. That's all there was to it."

Everything he tells you does not compute. "But, Freedo, how did you come back to life? I mean, if you ceased to exist, how did you get back to whatever you are? What are you now?"

"Let's say I'm a very active memory without any physical form. Calax III is on a rampage, searching the universe for a new crop of workers. Right now they're working on collecting Earthlings. So in order to fight them, I would need an Earth-form body. Do you think you can help me?"

"I don't know, Freedo. I don't really understand everything that's going on."

"It's very complex. But just trust me. If you don't want to help me take on an Earth-form body, it's okay. But come with me anyway—with your help I know Calax III can be defeated. What do you say?"

Turn to the next page.

Sensing urgency in Freedo's voice, you realize you need to make a decision quickly. There shouldn't be any harm in joining Freedo. In fact, this is your opportunity to finally meet him, face-to-face, and check out his world.

Suddenly, though, a thought occurs to you—this guy could be an impostor. It could be Calax III. Now things are really spinning in your head. If this is really Freedo, there's no way you can turn on him now. You've got to join him. But you don't necessarily have to help him take on an Earth-form body.

If you trust this guy to be Freedo and want to help him take on an Earth-form body, turn to page 72.

If you agree to join Freedo despite your skepticism that he might be an impostor, turn to page 78.

If you decide not to join Freedo and just stay put, turn to page 107.

"Okay, Aldo, old buddy, what is this secret pact business? I'm ready, but let's hurry," you say, already fearing Lepto's arrival.

Aldo smiles a kid-style smile of victory. "Follow me. Do exactly what I say. I mean exactly. Don't miss a step or a move, or you'll be sorry. This pact will give me some of Earth's powers and you some of my planet's powers."

Turn to the next page.

Aldo draws a pattern on the forest floor with a branch from one of the trees. Then he moves quickly and precisely in a series of steps that resembles a dance routine from an oldies sock hop. The Aldo Fitmouse you remember from third grade never moved with such grace. You follow him as best you can, but it isn't easy.

Finally he stops. "Okay, here's the hard part. You must join hands like this." He folds his arms into a complicated arm-wrestling hold. And when he unfolds them, he produces a silver cup. "Then we must drink from this cup."

The cup is filled with the most disgusting liquid you have ever seen or smelled. It looks like a failed biology experiment from your second-grade class on tadpole—frog growth.

"Yuck! I'm not drinking that," you say, revolted by the sight and smell of the liquid in the cup.

"Now or never. Lepto is coming," Aldo warns. He has already slurped up some of the foul stuff. A black dribble of fluid runs down his chin.

"Okay, here goes!" You raise the cup, put it to your lips, tip it ever so slightly, and pretend to drink.

Turn to the next page.

"You're cheating!" Aldo exclaims. "I can tell. Are all you Earthlings so dishonest and cowardly?"

"Hey, don't insult me. I didn't ask to come here," you fire back.

"Oh, yeah! Who says? You came here because you really wanted to, and don't deny it."

"Oh, yeah—prove it," you say, getting really angry.

"I can, and you'll be sorry," Aldo replies. You sense a deep threat in his tone. "I know about your own special pact with the Dark Force! I know you promised the Force your loyalty if only you could travel to other planets. Don't deny it. You asked for special, and I mean special, help."

"Hey, I was only kidding around. I didn't mean anything. And it wasn't the Dark Force anyway. I just wished really hard that I could search the planets for my friend Freedo. That's all. Nothing more."

"Don't get touchy. If you didn't want your mind to be read, you shouldn't have had those thoughts in the first place," Aldo says in a peevish voice. "Whether you know it or not, this place is a figment of your imagination. You created this, not me. But watch out. I hear old Lepto coming."

Go on to the next page.

The sound of drums and a rumbling of trains reverberate in the distance. The forest sky darkens as if a thunderstorm were approaching. The wind in the metallic branches increases. You glance at Aldo, tip the cup, and drink the evil-looking liquid.

"Ugh—this tastes like drainpipe water!" you exclaim.

At that very instant, Lepto arrives. Towering above the metallic trees, this monster creature looks like a blown-up version of the big bully who used to tease you at school.

"Run!" Aldo shouts. "The potion will give you super speed! Run!"

One last look at Lepto standing above you is all it takes. You command your feet to move.

"Coward!" Lepto thunders.

Lepto's slur hits home. How dare he call you a coward? you think. But it's obvious you're scared. He's testing you. He wants you to run away like a coward. And if you stay, he could put you through any sort of intolerable pain. Either way you're doomed, you think.

"Coward, coward, coward!" Lepto taunts.

If you stay and confront Lepto, turn to page 77.

If you run, turn to page 98.

You decide to stick it out. Late that night, under a carpet of stars, snuggled in your sleeping bag, you watch the heavens.

Your fire of gnarled pinyon smokes and crackles. The coals are comforting. Little heat is given, but the life of the fire soothes you.

Meanwhile, far out in the cosmos, your friend Freedo attempts to make contact once again. Freedo is racing against time . . . time and the forces of Calax III.

You sleep, and sometime near dawn you are awakened by two objects that appear in the thin light and approach the mesa.

They move slowly, as if dancing. You're excited—somehow you know one of them is Freedo. You prepare to greet them. You are a true Earth diplomat, and the connections you make with Freedo and his people benefit all living things for all time.

The End

"So how can I help you become like a human, Freedo? Is it going to be very different from what you are?" you ask.

"Yes and no. Essentially, an Earthling is a replicable life form that is made up of more than 70 percent water, some minerals, and other junk, and energized into life." Freedo pauses, then continues. "Where I come from, there is no water; we are assembled by a committee directed by elders, and we can be deactivated at any time."

"Can you have kids?" you ask.

"Not really. We can submit design specifications. We do develop a certain fondness for those we are involved with. But it isn't the same as it appears to be on Earth."

"Hm, that's sad. I mean not having your own family and people like brothers and sisters."

"Don't feel sorry for us. It's just a different way of life. There are other rewards. But I do envy you and your pleasant, simple lives."

"Simple! Are you crazy? Our lives aren't simple. Look at our world. You call that simple?" you demand, quite agitated.

"I apologize, my dear Earthling. Things rarely are as they appear. You just don't know how difficult things are where I come from."

"Well, enough of that. Let's see if we can get you into an Earthling body. Any preferences?" you ask.

Go on to the next page.

"Well, now that you ask, I do have some ideas," Freedo tells you.

"Let's hear them," you reply.

"Well, I was thinking that it might be nice to be an NBA basketball star, say playing for the Bullets or the Sonics. I rather like the size and form, and I really appreciate the way they fly."

"Well, you'd certainly be conspicuous in that form. Any other choices?" you ask hopefully.

"Yes, I think maybe a rap artist would be nice. Or how about one of your TV anchors?"

"Get real, Freedo. You're picking unrealistic Earth creatures. Can't you settle for a school kid with braces or a mom with three kids or something simple?" you suggest.

"But I want to experience what Earth is all about," Freedo pleads.

"I've got an idea, Freedo. Why don't you settle for a fourteen-year-old kid? Okay?"

"If you insist."

"Let's do it. But wait a minute. How?" you ask.

Turn to the next page.

"Caught you!" snarls Holly, entering the room armed with a strange-looking device. "Okay, Freedo, we knew this whiz kid would lead you to us. Don't migrate. Dardion is all around."

As you watch, Holly begins to change her form. Her skin sloughs off, revealing a scaly green covering. Her hair slips down over a metallic ball fitted with a row of shining lights. Her arms, legs, feet, and hands disappear. Before you hovers a terrifying and unique-looking creature, quivering with energy.

"Dardion may well be here, Suprana, but I did not come alone this time," Freedo says. "I've got Zippo waiting in the ether. Ready, Zippo?"

There is a slight moaning sound, probably Zippo replying in the affirmative.

You try to slip back, edging near the door.

Freedo speaks to you. "Go! Zippo and I are holding Suprana in a force field. You have 83 seconds to exit. Do not turn back. Hurry, you are on your own."

If you take advantage of the 83-second grace period, make tracks by turning to page 4.

If you decide to stay and help Freedo in his fight with this creature, turn to page 91

Gathering up every last ounce of belief in yourself, you stay put.

"I'm no coward, Lepto! You're a bully, and you know it. Bullies are the biggest cowards of all. Pick on someone your own size." You start marching straight for the giant feet. You are ready to fight.

As you advance, a strange and marvelous thing happens. You feel yourself expand—first your feet, then legs, then body and arms and hands, and finally your head. Within seconds you are towering above Lepto, who shrinks smaller and smaller until he is lost among the roots of the metallic trees.

Now your head is high above the forest, touching the clouds.

"Aldo, where are you?" you ask. Your voice is mellow and soft.

"What happened to you?" Aldo asks, peeping out from behind a metallic tree.

Turn to page 104.

"Sure, I'll join you, Freedo," you say.

"I knew you would. Great. Get ready. Hold very still. Try not to breathe. Now. . . ."

There is a humming sound, followed by a glimmer of purple light that bathes you in a coat of energy.

"Okay?" Freedo asks.

"Wait, what's going on?" you shout, but Freedo can't hear you over the buzz.

"Increasing power levels. Tell me if it's too much."

You feel a tingly electrical charge starting in your fingers. Slowly it reaches your head and then your toes.

"Be still. Hold very quiet. No movement." Freedo speaks in a calm and reassuring voice.

"Hey, it's beginning to hurt," you say, almost sure now that joining Freedo was a deadly choice.

"What?" yells Freedo.

"My skin is stretching. Or my bones are shrinking. My brain feels like it's on fire. Yikes! Help!"

"Too much—sorry. But we're at a point of no return. If we stop now, you could be permanently damaged. If we go ahead, you'll probably make it. Can you stand more?"

If you decide to stop now, turn to page 121.

If you decide to go ahead and risk it, turn to page 99.

You decide to flee from Aldo as fast as you can. This is getting too weird for words. You don't know what lurks in the metallic forest—but you're ready for anything as long as it has nothing to do with Aldo.

"So long, Aldo. Have a nice life!" you say, heading off into the deep forest.

"Wait! Wait for me! Don't leave me alone! Please!" Aldo begs.

You stop short, wondering what he wants. Maybe he truly means you no harm. Maybe he'll stop the silly games.

If you decide to let Aldo catch up with you, turn to page 115.

If you decide to leave Aldo to his own fate, turn to page 96.

You decide to confide in Holly. But first you want to figure out how much she knows.

"So what makes you think I'm hiding something?" you ask.

"Well, why do you think you're here?"

Now you're really confused. She's not giving you the answers you want. And you know she won't let you in on anything until you give in. "Well, I was in contact with a friend named Freedo," you say cautiously. You want to remain fairly vague so you don't give too much away. If she knows anything about Freedo, she'll fully understand. Otherwise you can make up some phony story.

"I was afraid of that. Don't ever mention that name again," she says, moving several steps closer to you. She peers into your face and asks, "Who sent you?" Her voice is steel cold.

"No one. Honest, no one," is your reply.

"We will see about that. Come this way," she says.

Go on to the next page.

You follow her out of your office and down the corridor. There is no one else in the research center. Your footsteps echo down the hallway. As you enter an elevator, Holly pushes the button for the basement. You remember that is where the old electronic equipment is stored. Pitt also told you the basement was off-limits for security reasons— top secret information is kept there.

Turn to the next page.

Once you reach the basement, Holly punches in a special code on the digital lock of a vaultlike door. There is a moment of silence, then a humming followed by a piercing light beacon. The heavy door slides easily, and you are propelled forward into space. The door slides back. You see nothing but blackness. Holly is gone.

The room grows hotter by the moment. You can feel the walls beginning to glow. Your skin is drying out rapidly. Your eyes feel like sandpaper. You crave water. Your throat is parched. You try to scream, but the sound is locked in your throat.

A pencil line of light far to your right beams across your face. But the heat seems to be coming from that direction. Looking up, you notice a glass, mirrorlike surface. You make out a knob that strangely seems to be attached to the mirrored ceiling.

If you decide to go to the light, turn to page 87.

If you decide to reach for the knob on the ceiling, turn to page 109.

A panel in the velvet opens, and five thin, silver, pointed-headed beings with single eyes and reed-like ears enter the room. Their arms and legs are strawlike. They look very similar to the typical aliens described in UFO sightings.

You imagine that Earthlings are subjects of great interest to these supposed extraterrestrial observers. Often those who claim to have had encounters with crews like this return unharmed but unhappy. Many feel that they have been subjected to detailed examinations, the way a new species of animal would be, after being found by some expedition. You hope this won't happen to you.

Turn to the next page.

"Hey, you guys, hold off a moment," you say. "I'd like to talk with you or someone in command. Please send in your boss."

Your words catch them by surprise. They jabber in what sounds like a cross between the churning of a washing machine and a DVD player skipping and blurting. They seem confused and agitated.

They disappear as suddenly as they appeared. The velvet on the wall where the panel opened up is now back in place. There is no mark to indicate that there ever was such an entrance or exit.

As you search the walls, you stumble across a small golden object. Without touching it, you examine the device. On Earth it would be thought to be a key. Up here, who knows what it is? A faint glow comes from the object. You wonder if it could be radioactive. Maybe it's some kind of test.

Suddenly, you feel yourself being watched. Maybe the walls are one-way velvet mirrors, and the robots are watching your every move. You're frightened and don't know what to do.

If you decide to pick up the "key,"
turn to page 113.

If you decide to ignore it, turn to page 105.

Despite the fact that the light also seems to be the source of the heat, you are somehow attracted to it.

Slowly, as if walking in your sleep, you move toward the light. But at each step you feel held back by some strange resistance. Painfully you lift each foot and finally get it back to the floor.

"You are making a mistake," comes a sonorous voice from behind you. "It is not too late to turn back."

The heat intensifies, and you feel the clothes on your body begin to scorch, as if they had just been removed from beneath an iron. Perspiration flows through your pores. Your eyes sting from salty fluids.

You go on, ignoring the voice. Bit by bit, the light grows larger. The heat continues to intensify.

"I'm warning you! Stop! Stop, now!" the voice says.

Turn to the next page.

Continuing onward, you feel the resistance on your feet ease up. You begin to run, not out of fear but out of excitement and anticipation. A long tunnel stretches out before you. The heat is now less, almost pleasant.

The tunnel opens up.

You are standing in a large field filled with thousands of ancient and modern flying machines, from gull-winged, fragile wooden contraptions to glowing orbs of translucent material.

No one else is in the field. Calmness and a sense of freedom surround you.

You are drawn to a peculiar, insectlike object. Thin, finlike wings stick out from its cylinder body.

"Enter. We have been waiting," comes a voice.

Turn to the next page.

"Freedo! It's you!" you exclaim.

"Of course. I told you to be patient."

Moments later you and Freedo and a small band of others begin a long journey to the outer belt of the Ragullian Galaxy.

"Calax III is tough. They almost got you, didn't they?" Freedo says. "I've been watching, unable to interfere, until you followed the light. I'm so glad we've found each other at last. Now we can concentrate on defeating them. Are you ready?"

The End

"I'm staying, Freedo. No way am I leaving you here."

"A very foolish move, my young Earthworm," Suprana says. The green, scaly surface of her oddly shaped body now sheds its scales and becomes a shiny metallic surface. It seems to radiate heat.

"Don't listen to Suprana," Freedo commands.

"No, don't listen to Freedo. You Earthlings don't know the first thing about any of us. You all insist on learning the hard way. Don't you get it? Freedo and I might be from different sectors of the cosmos, but we are the same. We are here on this stupid little planet to cultivate a brand-new colony. You are in our power."

While Suprana is babbling away, you are able to sneak back to the computer and gain access to the data bank. You bring up Alien Life forms on the screen and begin a search.

"Hey, away from the computer, Earthworm," Suprana shouts.

Turn to the next page.

You do not move, hoping that Freedo will intervene. This will be the big test. Will he show the true colors of a friend, or has Freedo been using you all along?

"Access Extraterrestrial Calax III," Freedo says.

You search the menu and click on Extraterrestrial Calax III. A box opens up and offers a short profile on these inhabitants of a remote galactic zone many millions of light-years from Earth. Skimming the text, you stumble on a section that reads:

> Calax III inhabitants are weakened by use of daylight simulators. Their underdeveloped pineal glands become overstimulated and they are returned to a state of relative harmlessness.

"Do it!" Freedo says. "I can't hold on much longer. I've got Suprana in a mind net, but it's weakening quickly. Do it!"

Go on to the next page.

"Okay, okay!" you reply. Your only trouble is to find a daylight simulator. But then you realize all you need is light. Any old light will do as long as it's not the light from a computer. You remember that Holly always wore tinted glasses.

You move to the wall switches. There are five of them in a neat little row right by the door.

"Don't do it," Suprana pleads, and for a moment you hesitate. Then slowly you reach up and push the first switch, then the next and the next until the whole room is flooded in bright, harsh light.

Turn to the next page.

Suprana seems to shudder, shrink, and become smaller by increments. Loud sobbing fills the room. Near the desk where the computer stands, you become aware of a faint outline. As Suprana shrinks, the outline begins to fill in, part by part.

"I'm doing it!" Freedo says.

Suddenly a blurry, humanoid being stands before you. It's Freedo! Instinctively you both reach to shake hands. As you are about to make contact, Freedo's new Earth-form dissolves.

"This is enough for tonight, my young friend. Tell no one. Let's go back to your home. I want to really experience the Earthling life. I won't cause any trouble."

Years later, the Nobel Prize for physics is awarded to you for advanced space and life studies. Thanks to Freedo, you've been able to contribute valuable knowledge that has widely increased tolerance for all forms of life.

The End

"Too bad, Aldo, but I've got places to go, things to do, and hopefully real people to see," you reply, not letting up your pace. Aldo's voice becomes distant, sounding more like a mosquito buzzing than anything else.

You increase your speed, zooming over tree roots, squinching around huge metallic tree trunks. The forest gets thicker and thicker. Little or no light penetrates the canopy of leaves. There is an eerie silence.

Your breath heaves in short, agonizing bursts. Your lungs feel on fire. But you push on and on, running aimlessly now.

Crash! You smash into a huge tree that seems to have just leaped out in your way.

"YOU'LL NEVER ESCAPE!" Oddly, the voice is in your brain. "THERE IS NO ESCAPE FROM THIS WORLD!"

You fight to hold back tears of fear and frustration. You run and run, as if there is nothing else to do. No alternatives, no hope, no future.

"Yikes! Where did you come from?" you ask as you almost stumble across Aldo, who is sitting in the middle of the forest. Tears cascade down his face.

Go on to the next page.

"I thought you'd never come back," Aldo cries out. "I thought you'd left me."

"Well, here I am," you say. You're not sure if you've returned to where you left Aldo, or if Aldo has used some of his magical powers to appear before you. Either way, you're confused, but you don't want Aldo to know it. "So, where is old Lepto, anyway? I don't see or hear him anymore," you say.

"He got bored and left. He told me I'd get it some other time. He means it, too," Aldo says, his tears drying.

"So what do you want?" you ask.

"Well, I was wondering. If I try my very best to reverse the experiment, can I come with you back to Earth? Please?"

Turn to page 115.

98

You run with all your might, legs pounding, arms pumping, gasping for breath. The faster you run, the closer Lepto seems to get. Just when he's right on your heels and about to crush you, you get a burst of speed. His big toe just grazes you. Soon you're way ahead of him. But then you realize you're right on his heels. You're running in circles! Slow down, you think—but not too much, or he'll catch up.

"What can I do, Aldo?" you cry out.

"Overcome your fear," he answers.

Easier said than done. "Aldo! Help me!" you cry out again. There is no reply.

You're tired; you can't take it anymore. You stop. Lepto lets out a huge bellowing laugh.

Turn to page 102.

You decide to go ahead and risk continuing Freedo's experiment. You can bear the pain, but you hope you haven't been too impulsive. If this guy is an impostor, you're now easy prey.

The pain increases. You feel your bones creak and groan under the strain, which seems like a rapid increase in gravity. Your blood thickens to the consistency of a heavy, coarse soup. It is sluggish in your veins, which are contracting. Your capillaries scream for relief.

Suddenly, you feel a shift of energy.

Turn to the next page.

"Freedo, I made it!" you exclaim, exiting the purple light. You step out into a sun-filled world that reflects a million images of radiant flowers in all stages of growth. You hear water—the roar of the sea and the coursing of a stream. No clouds obscure the deep yellow sky.

"What now, Freedo?" you ask. Looking down at your body, you notice you are wearing a garment of the finest material you have ever come across. It appears to be made of ground seashells.

"Relax, my friend. Relax. We are about to start our journey back to Mydeeradon, at the center of the known universe. You will be welcomed there. You are only the third creature from Earth that we have ever successfully brought back."

"Why me?" you ask.

"You were chosen. You are a superb specimen—intelligent, courageous, and just. Now away we must go."

"But what about Calax III?" you ask.

"We'll worry about that later. Let's go celebrate. I want you to meet all my friends and see my home."

The End

"I've got you now," he shouts, and the metallic trees wither at the sound of his voice.

You hear a humming sound, low, soft, but persistent. On instinct you turn toward it. There in the base of a giant metal tree trunk is an opening. The sound is coming from the opening. You step cautiously forward. The nearer you get, the louder the humming becomes. Now it sounds like the buzz of a million bees.

"Open the door!" comes a command from far in the distance.

Go on to the next page.

For a moment you hesitate.

Lepto moves ponderously forward, backward, and sideways. The light of the sun is blocked. Darkness fills the forest.

"I've got you, you pint-sized coward," Lepto says scornfully.

Ignoring him, you force yourself to move. You grasp the handle of the door in the tree trunk. A sudden flash of light, along with a swarm of escaping metallic bees, knocks you down. Millions of them fill the air and rush to attack Lepto. He screams in agony. "Let me go!"

It is too late for Lepto—the metallic bees have got him. It's horrifying to watch—now you really wish you could help the pitiful creature. And with this wish comes an idea: you can divert the bees by attacking their nest.

Turn to page 120.

"I just found my strength. I don't have to be afraid of old Lepto, or any bullies. And neither do you."

Lepto doesn't wait around to find out about your plans for him. Actually you hadn't planned to do anything to Lepto—you're no bully. But you do feel a twinge of delight when you realize that he was frightened enough to flee. No one had ever stood up to Lepto. To Aldo, you're a magical hero.

It's time to go home. Before Aldo zaps you back to Earth, you make another secret pact, one in which you promise to embark on another space adventure with him sometime soon—once you find Freedo.

The End

You move as far away from the golden object as you can, bumping into the velvet wall across from it. Then you wait. And wait.

The wait seems interminable. You doze off, dreaming of home and school and all your friends. You remember birthdays, holidays off from school, the Fourth of July, and great days with your closest friends. Even the grim days that you had hoped to forget are now vivid memories.

Every time you try to block a dream or a memory from coming up, you feel a gentle electronic probe to your brain.

Yikes! You are being invaded. Your mind is being searched. You must be under examination.

The lights go out. You sleep.

Turn to the next page.

"Freedo? Freedo? Is that you? Is that really you?" you ask, waking up. You are fearful that you are asleep and that this is all a terrible dream.

"Yes. It is me. I've been waiting for you for a long time. I knew you'd be picked up by the search team. They are looking for the best they can find on Earth. You are one of the best. You've passed all the tests. I think you are the last one to be gathered. I think they will return now. They have a full load."

"Where am I going?"

"Back to the center of the universe. I'll see you soon."

The End

"I'm sorry, Freedo. I just can't go with you."

"What do you mean? You're my last hope. You can't do this to me," Freedo pleads.

"I'm just an ordinary kid, Freedo. As much as I would love to venture out into the unknown, I'm scared," you admit.

"Oh, you're just like the rest of them. You humans are such cowards. No sense of adventure. So satisfied with the humdrum. Sorry, but I need to move on—find someone to help me. Thanks—it's been real."

As you leave your office and head back to your room, you feel a little sad. If that was the real Freedo, you let him down. You wonder if you'll ever speak to him again.

Once you fall asleep, you begin to dream of all the long, wonderful conversations you had with Freedo. Suddenly, his words—"Help me!"—stick in your mind, like the sound of a broken record. You start twisting and turning to the rhythm of his cries. An image of a blur, also twisting and turning, appears. It's like a tornado of stars. As it continues to spiral more violently, the cries become louder and louder. Suddenly the image blows up into nothing. The cries are interrupted by a high-pitched screeching sound. Then, finally, silence.

Turn to the next page.

That was years ago. Since then you have relived that dream in your sleep over and over. You have never heard from Freedo again, but you will never stop mourning the loss of a very valuable friend.

The End

Responding to some powerful internal force, you reach up and grab for the knob in the mirror-like ceiling.

"I can just make it," you say, stretching to your full extension.

"That's right. Just turn the knob," comes a soft voice.

Finally you grasp the knob.

Zark!

There is a flash of light and a sucking sound like a giant toilet being flushed. You are drawn up into a vortex of great strength and wrapped in coils of purple energy.

"What's happening?" you scream.

Turn to the next page.

Your cry is not answered.

Minutes fly by, and the vortex carries you up and away from Earth. You are aware of transiting galaxies, of crossing vast space and even time. Throughout the journey you hear a consistent sound, something researchers on Earth call the Music of the Spheres.

Back on your birth planet, several researchers in different facilities from Australia to Colorado to Russia note the presence of a signal that seems to be of human origin. It is your transit across the universe. Your destination is unknown.

Little does anyone know, Calax III has added another specimen to its collection of galactic life forms.

The End

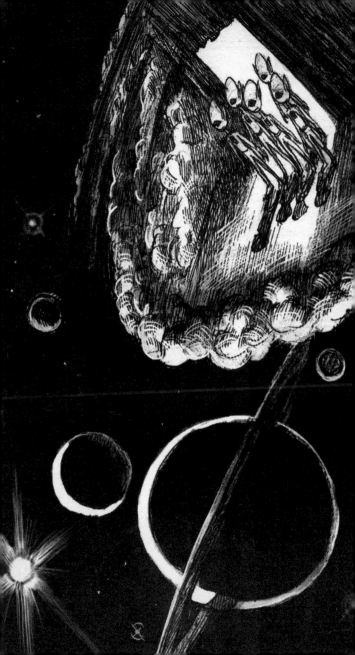

You can't resist the temptation to pick up the golden object. It might be your last "key" to freedom. You move ever so slowly toward it and stoop to reach for it.

"Yabba! Yabba!" you hear. A cry of victory or despair? From whom?

Although you're confused, you ignore the cry. The golden object fits snugly in your hand. You walk to the far wall, scan the velvet, and discover the doorway. Opening it with the golden object, you are swept away into eternity!

The End

"Okay, Aldo," you tell him. "I'll let you come with me. But from now on I'm the leader. No more fussing around. I've had it with this planet and your experiments, and with Lepto. I'll tell you one thing—if this is some giant cosmic joke, you're wasting my time. I've got things to do and a friend to locate."

"Of course, of course. I'll do anything you say. Just get me away from Lepto."

"Great idea, Aldo. But just how do we leave this moldy old rock? You brought me here. You take me back home."

"I can't. I mean . . . I want to, but it isn't so easy as that. You have to do it yourself," Aldo explains.

"Oh, I get it. This is supposed to be one of those big tests. I'm supposed to show maturity and leadership, right? Well, all I'm showing is the need to escape. So get moving. This way!" You dash off into the thickest part of the forest.

The trees begin to unfold their branches, creating a tunnel. A white light gleams at the end of the tunnel. You run faster than you ever have in your life, hoping that the light in the distance represents a safe place.

Turn to the next page.

"Hurry, Aldo! We can't play around!" you yell.

"I'm hurrying, I'm hurrying. I'm just not as fast as you. I can't run as hard."

"Well, you're going to have to, Aldo, or Lepto will get us both." You push on, and Aldo plods along behind you.

The going isn't easy. The trees get thicker and thicker. The white light seems just as far away as it was the first time you saw it.

Stop! Stop!

A familiar voice thunders through the trees.

"Don't listen!" Aldo almost screams. "Ignore it!"

"Don't worry, Aldo. I'm tired of obeying everyone else. We're out of here."

The forest floor suddenly opens up beneath you, and you and Aldo tumble down through a void like falling leaves.

Turn to the next page.

Your fear vanishes. The speed of your fall slows. Your memory of Lepto and the strange planet dims. Aldo grows fainter and fainter, fading into barely a blur.

You relax, enjoying the trip, enjoying the slow, featherlike drop.

Go on to the next page.

Bright lights glare above you. Unfamiliar voices buzz in your ears.

"Blood pressure dropping. Pulse light and erratic. I think we're losing—"

"No, we're not. C'mon, you can do it," you hear. It's Freedo!

"Freedo!" you shout. With a massive effort, you bring yourself back to life, back to reality.

"I can't believe it. Pulse is up. Blood pressure is rising. This kid is coming back."

Your recovery is fairly fast, but you still wonder about what really happened. Some say you were hit by a car outside the research facility; others say you fainted and hit your head on the curb. The only thing you feel sure of is that both you and Freedo are safe.

The End

From a distance you hurl several rocks into the nest. It works! Lepto is quickly freed from his tormentors. Oddly, he begins to shrink until he reaches your height. With tears welling, he looks you straight in the eyes. "Thank you," he says humbly.

You feel a sense of warmth and goodness. Lepto just stands there, waiting for a response, and you realize he's never looked so vulnerable. You don't know what to say.

Reluctantly, Lepto offers you his hand. Smiling, you reach to shake it. Once your hands meet—poof!—Lepto's gone. Instantly you realize that he's zapped you back to Earth.

The End

"Stop! Stop, Freedo. I can't stand it." Your brain is frying.

"Okay, I'll stop. I hope you will be all right." The pain eases. Your brain cools down. The purple light recedes.

"Freedo! Freedo! Where are you?" you yell. There is no reply. You have no sense of space or motion. Your only hope is that Freedo will be able to undo the changes. But perhaps your instincts were right—maybe Freedo was an imposter. Maybe you're being held captive by Calax III. It seems as if you'll never know the real truth.

The End

CREDITS

Illustrator: Vladimir Semionov was born in August 1964 in the Republic of Moldavia, of the former USSR. He is a graduate of the Fine Arts Collegium in Kishinev, Moldavia, as well as the Fine Arts Academy of Romania, where he majored in graphics and painting, respectively. He has had exhibitions all over the world, in places like Japan and Switzerland, and is currently Art Director of the SEM&BL Animacompany animation studio in Bucharest.

Cover Artist: Marco Cannella was born in Ascoli Piceno, Italy, on September 29, 1972. Marco started his career in art as decorator and illustrator when he was a college student. He became a full-time professional in 2001 when he received the flag-prize for the "Palio della Quintana" (one of the most important Italian historical games). Since then, he has worked as illustrator for the Studio Inventario in Bologna. He has also worked as scenery designer for professional theater companies. He works for the production company ASP sril in Rome as character designer and set designer on the preproduction of a CG feature film. In 2004, he moved to Bangalore, India, to work full-time on this project as art director.

This book was brought to life by a great group of people:

Shannon Gilligan, Publisher

Gordon Troy, General Counsel

Melissa Bounty, Senior Editor

Stacey Boyd, Designer

Kris Town and Cait Close, Proofreaders

ABOUT THE AUTHOR

R. A. MONTGOMERY has hiked in the Himalayas, climbed mountains in Europe, scuba-dived in Central America, and worked in Africa. He lives in France in the winter, travels frequently to Asia, and calls Vermont home. Montgomery graduated from Williams College and attended graduate school at Yale University and NYU. His interests include macro-economics, geo-politics, mythology, history, mystery novels, and music. He has two grown sons, a daughter-in-law, and two granddaughters. His wife, Shannon Gilligan, is an author and noted interactive game designer. Montgomery feels that the new generation of people under 15 is the most important asset in our world.

Visit us online at CYOA.com for games and other fun stuff, or to write to R. A. Montgomery!

Introduces

The Golden Path

A three-book interactive epic story.
There is more than one way to get
from one book to the next,
but only one Golden Path.

FROM: Dianna Torman
dtorman@deadmail.anonymous.guyana.000
SUBJECT: Something has happened to us.

Sweetheart, I don't want to alarm you, but I fear I must. If you are getting this email it is because something has happened to us. It is rigged to be sent from a special "dead drop" anonymous server if I have not checked back in three days. Your father and I have been afraid that people were moving against us after we were removed from heading the Carlsbad dig. I can't get too specific because I do not know myself who exactly is targeting us. We will try and contact you as soon as we are able.

Leave school and go see your Uncle Harry in Carlsbad. He works in the branch office of the Federal Historical Accuracy Board and he can help you. His work address is: FHAB District Office, Harold Turner, 224 Mesa Street, Suite B11, Carlsbad, NM.

Don't call him or email him, just go see him as soon as possible!

Use the flyer at home if you can. It has enough fuel to get to Carlsbad, and its transponder codes have been authorized to fly there. Don't try going anywhere else though, as the Gatekeepers will immediately stop you. They keep a tight leash on all flyers.

Rimy can give you a ride home from school; he is a trusted friend. Just tell him I asked him as a "special boon."

I will try and leave a more detailed note in the secret spot. There is much your father and I need to explain to you, but I can't really explain until I see you in person. I can't wait until I see your beautiful face! Be strong, be brave, and know that your father and I love you more than life itself! I am sorry to scare you with this news, but it will all work out in the end!!!!

Love,
Mom

"I think I'm going to be sick," you moan as soon as you finish your mom's email. Maybe this is just some big joke? But Tito's death is no joke, and nothing about this day has been very funny. "I don't even have an 'Uncle Harry.'"

The phone rings and all three of you jump. You look at the caller ID, and it says: Billings, Palmer and Polk.

"It's my parents' financial advisor. He calls all the time, but why would he be calling at midnight?"

"Hello?" you say into the mouthpiece.

"It's Preston Billings here, are your parents home? I need to talk to Dianna or Donald immediately."

"No, Mr. Billings, they're not here. I don't know where they are. I think they are in trouble." Billings has always been nice to you, but you don't know why you tell him that.

"What do you mean in trouble?" he asks. "They were on their way to meet me here tonight. In New York City. But they never showed up. God! I hate that they outlawed cell phones. All for safety!" He gives a bitter laugh.

"Why were they coming to meet you?" you ask.

"I think it would be best if you came here to New York City. I have some new information for your parents that is very important to all of you."

"I think someone has taken them," you say weakly, voicing your fear for the first time. "We found my mom's dog Tito dead in their workshop. The house is...neat but everything just seems strange."

There's a long pause.

"Honestly, I think you need to get out of there right now," Mr. Billings says urgently. "I can arrange a travel document via email. Do you have a car?"

"Yes," you answer. Peter and Dresdale are staring at you with intense eagerness, but they are keeping silent and following your lead. You haven't mentioned them yet. "Mr. Billings, I am not sure

should tell you this, but my mom sent an email that would only
e triggered if they were in trouble. I just read it. She says I need to
o meet with someone in Calsbad, some friend of theirs."

"Don't go to Carlsbad!" he says. "Not with the explosion. It's is
oo dangerous now! Listen, give me your email address and I'll send
he travel documents in the morning. Right now I want you to get
ut of there."

"Why?" you ask. You have a flashback to that afternoon when
ou first saw the tall figure of Dr. Schlieman.

"I really can't talk over the phone," Billings replies. "Please take
my word for it. I'll email you the documents. Get out of there as
quickly as possible."

The phone line goes dead.

You are stunned. Things seem to be moving fast, and in the
wrong direction. You look at your two friends.

"What do we do? This flyer your mom mentioned in her email,
how did they get it?" Peter asks.

"The government gave them a low level flyer for the excavation
they did in Belize. They didn't use it much at the Carlsbad dig. It
should fit the three of us with room for half a toothbrush."

"What did that Billings guy say?" Dresdale asks.

"He said we should get out of here as soon as possible and go
to New York City to meet him. He says he has information for my
parents. They were scheduled to be there to meet him tonight. He
also said 'don't go to Carlsbad.'" Your head pulses with a weary
ache, but your heart and stomach feel much worse

"I hate to say this, but I am going to faint if I don't get some
food," says Peter. Dresdale glares at him. "What?" he asks defen-
sively. "I haven't eaten since we had mac and cheese at the dining
hall for lunch."

"No, you're right. We need to get some food, and get out of
here," you say. "But where do we go?"

"Can you operate the flyer?" Dresdale asks.

"It's mostly automated, but my dad let me take it into manua mode a couple of times. You don't get very high off the ground an if the power quits it has a backup elevation field that brings yo down easy. Where do you guys think I should go?"

"What do you mean, 'I'?" says Dresdale. "We're coming wit you."

"Yeah," agrees Peter. "But after we get some food!"

"These are my problems. You two should go to Dresdale' Mom's house" you reply. "I've gotten you in enough trouble. I' take care of this."

"Don't be nuts. We're not going to let you go off by yoursel Anyway, I'm not sure what is going on, but somehow I think tha we are all in this together," Dresdale says, and her face looks s earnest and caring that you feel almost good for a second. The reality comes crashing down again.

"So where are we going? Do we listen to the email from m mom and take the flyer or listen to Billings and go to the Big Sogg Apple?"

If you choose to follow your mother's plea in the dead-drop emai and go to Carlsbad to meet "Uncle Harry", turn to page 43

If your gut tells you to go to New York City to meet Preston Billing and learn his "important information", turn to page 36